Formless

Dibyasree Nandy

Ukiyoto Publishing

All global publishing rights are held by

Ukiyoto Publishing

Published in 2023

Content Copyright © Dibyasree Nandy

ISBN 9789360168438

*All rights reserved.
No part of this publication may be reproduced,
transmitted, or stored in a retrieval system, in any
form by any means, electronic, mechanical,
photocopying, recording or otherwise, without the
prior permission of the publisher.*

The moral rights of the authors have been asserted.

*This is a work of fiction. Names, characters,
businesses, places, events, locales, and incidents are
either the products of the author's imagination or
used in a fictitious manner. Any resemblance to
actual persons, living or dead, or actual events is
purely coincidental.*

*This book is sold subject to the condition that it shall
not by way of trade or otherwise, be lent, resold,
hired out or otherwise circulated, without the
publisher's prior consent, in any form of binding or
cover other than that in which it is published.*

www.ukiyoto.com

Formless

Formless, without a shadow,
My palms empty, life drifts by as a butterfly's whim,
Give me a brush, a blade that chisels,
To illuminate the world, to carve,
One single stroke, an inky crescent moon.

~~

The edge of the petal severe, stern,
A silhouette, the sun at midnight pearly,
Beneath the small shade of the one tree, safe I am,
It burns, scorches, all aflame,
Heart imprisoned, a steely cage,
Fragile, brittle are sentiments, like autumnal leaves.
An honest hand extended, blistered, wounded,
The fire put out, the branches uprooted.

~~

The star falls to the sea,

The universe crumbles, grey rain tumbles,

Washed away is the title on the grave

Long lashes, beautiful, closed over turquoise eyes,

Roaring waves crash, a voiceless name.

~~

One, like a farewell of tears

Two, like loneliness and whispers of aid

Three, like pain, fear and despair

Four, the seasons etched into the irises, ever-shifting

The clock freezes, the pages of the era fly.

~~

The drooping willow, shrivelled as an old man's will,

Encircled by streaks of gold, castle of lightning

A day when the sky weeps, the earth burns with hellfire,

Chrysanthemums turn to ash, the trunk yet steadfast,

Reposing till the end of time, roots still standing.

~~

Spilling, the river of ruby at late dusk,

Rising, the breaths of a sooty, choking town,
The rushing wind past trees in winter,
Screams and wails, the banner of war ripped,
The ashen horse whinnying.

~~

Cogs of the world rusted,
The weights on the balance scale light,
Wings of the angel unfurled, a sword unsheathed,
None can be purged.

~~

A boat upon a brook of petals,
Blossoms from the heavens descend,
Blessing on the journey towards Death.

~~

Lilies he held dear,
For each life was twisted,
Shards of the crystalline, warped world sting like thorns,
As a pained rose he blooms.

~~

The planets move,

They come close, drift away,

Yet parallel are the oceans and the moon,

Like a lover who awaits.

~~

It perches atop a cliff,

The raven near the foggy waters,

In a flurry of black feathers, demise arrives.

~~

Like a cicada shell left behind, the dark castle,

The youthful emperor marches with a burning blade of white,

A trapped bird with hidden plumes, a prison of peace,

Promises of luck; the unfettered, belligerent crane takes flight.

~~

Camellias in the courtyard, the twilight sky without clouds,

The heart murky, without colour,

For the eyes reflect only swirling breeze,

The wind following a straying stalk of grain.

~~

Fumes from a golden pipe dance,

The mind in a vengeful haze

Moths on his garb flutter, the candle in the wick attracting,

The vessel headed towards the torrent

Life tossed down.

~~

Shades of the pigeon's breast obscured by rain's daze,

The gloom of hydrangeas' dew,

Memories blotted, a blank parchment

Recollections reshaped by autumn's blaze,

The book pristine as morning snow.

~~

Flakes of snow, rims sharp

Stinging, the tip of an icy blade

A pair of footmarks deep…

Standing beneath the dark sky, unloved.

~~

Your morality, a blade

Your honour, an attire finest

Your ideals, a shield with a regal crest

A blindfold over my eyes

I can envision a silhouette.

~~

Steadfast as brown,

Warm as amber,

A young face peach-tinted, tossed into a storm,

The topaz bursts to flame,

Like a chestnut trunk, many an axe he can brave.

~~

The sun, infantile

Pens a script of ruby red

Parchment of a new dawn

A bloodied book

Too grimy, the water melts to nothingness before its charred form.

~~

I have but one wing

Antithesis of an angel of gold

Writhing at the bottom of the sun-lit tower

My voice turns cold.

~~

O Patriot, what do your blazing eyes see?

A nation draped in misery

O Demon, what do your hands feel?

The desire to rip apart the last dregs of evil akin to me

O Angel, why do your wings unfold?

To depart in peace after my cleansing spree.

~~

Life choked out of a rose

The sunflower droops

An immaculate lily is set on fire

Hands of people, muddy.

~~

Before the mirror, no one by my side

A lonely image seen,

If I were to shatter the glass

Fragmented forms of me,

A bleeding soul of good fortune

Companions many.

~~

Imprisoned by love
Weighed down by faith
On the floor, praying
Speared by hope
We forget to inhale.

~~

Many pieces conjoined
An outline eludes
Confusion ensues,
Withdraw, consider
There, an object clear
Lucidity in synthesis.

~~

The trees whisper many a secret,
The wind, the messenger,
Blades are the grassy stems…
The fog curtains,
Despair takes root,
Shadows of old phantoms…
Boughs ensnare,

A constricted throat.

~~

The moonlit porch, the door to my dream

Tranquil, embraced by the breeze

Yet, the pale wisteria overhangs alone

Rippling stream afar,

A night to share a drink

But a petal settles on an empty cup, no guests approach, no nocturnal birds sing.

~~

A drizzle of flakes, a mantle of pearl

The moon, the stars obscured

Flickering lamps fade, flowers lose their hues

Silhouettes of silver come close

The bridge over the crystal waters aflame.

~~

Your feet reflected in the puddles as I walk in the rain

Your retreating back as I look behind

You sit against the opposite end of the tree trunk as I lean

Your shadow mine.

We cross blades as both howl in pain

We run swords through the other's chest

Both victims, we try to ease another's pain

Cowards we are, we know not how to wipe our own tears

Afraid of our own fears.

~~

"You look splendid, my king."

"What meaning is there in my new throne if the head-rest is not your lap

If the arm-rests are not your palms?"

"My place is but at your feet."

"What would your answer be if I held you close, by my side,

Not below, not above; my strength, my breath for eternity?"

~~

Strands falling across the face, just the lips seen, a burning rose,

All else grey,

A fair finger outstretched, a dragonfly of afternoon perched,

The buzzing of the gossamer wings, a medley with my heart,

As treacherous as summer's thunder.

~~

Like the stork departing; away, away from the orange river,

Should twilight descend for you in late autumn,

I will sleep beside you in winter, frozen,

Until spring's ripeness returns.

~~

Wine of opulence and ill-begotten wealth, carmine

Spills over the lily, tainted with a sickly shine

Lifted by the angel, it becomes a thorny rose, prickling

The demon's finger bleeding

Empty heavens, deserted hell

Night and day become one in a ballroom of mist.

~~

Forbidden to open my eyes, I hold the unbroken balance scale

Familiar faces once I can see, shattered is equality

For, in the dark, I know morality.

Formless

~~

The shawl stolen by the wind
Caught by an unsure identity,
The boat sets sail across the sea of memories
The oar shifting history.

~~

As fine as spider webs
Many paths forked
He who sits higher than the clouds
Counts every mistake.

~~

Blistered skin, fingers numb
I can only turn away
Loftier than the lune you are
Beautiful if seen through the mirror's other end.
Like a tiny petal being carried by the current's rapid flow
I shall drift into a nameless future of solitary days.

~~

Skeletal life
Flesh of death

The wind, a chain

Binding, encircling

We die before we are born

Our birth precedes death

The firebird that wakes, ashen.

Nothing moves forward

Nothing recedes

We are devoid of limbs

A mutilated soul, a noose around our neck.

Without courage we are but corpses

Even in pain, we take one step ahead, our time rotates.

~~

The sand deceptive, it hides the jagged edges of shells

The candle treacherous, making all shine before concealing

The riverbank of falsehood, the quagmire that swallows

Blossoms of cherry pink, enticing before fleeting

The lake of lies, reflecting that which we cannot touch,

A world of sin; reality, a fable
Only in nightmares can you see the truth.

~~

Sinews hurting, wrists tired
The art gifts fresh air
Yet he sees fangs slobbering, leering teeth
Those without faces who impale from behind.

~~

Embellished by the future
Twisted is the past
Ravenous is the future
Consumed is the past
Even if the archives are torn
The following moment kneels before the hour just passed.

~~

An encounter of fate
A teacher, a student, both are lost
Drawn together like celestial bodies
Like magnets seeking poles
A sanctuary, a temple of growth.

The pupil learns with wisdom

The mentor imparts erudition in awe

Searching for the path correct,

The wee child holding the tutor's hand

Together they walk towards the horizon

Rice-fields lining, the sun accompanying to the north.

~~

A wrinkle in the fabric of time

A moment etched into the heart,

Smoothed out is the fabric of time

Eternity; promises of eons that flow.

~~

Blue, loathsome

The sky brings joy

White, so familiar

Icicles that pierce

Black, my blood that runs dark

I survived amidst hateful green

A peaceful hamlet untouched by cannons that reduced all to dust.

~~

Bones of ivory

A mane of porcelain

The collapsed creature alone at the edge of the world

A frosted carpet of glistening diamonds

The last sight seen, the death of the earth

Blooming moonflowers in an emerald paradise.

~~

Walking in the dark by my lonesome, I wished for a voice to reach me

Only a shrill quietude

But a swallow-tailed butterfly brushed past my cheek

A white shadow behind

Who goes there? I ask

My words still cannot touch you? They sadly say, Open your eyes.

~~

I look to my right with a smile, there is a raging tundra

I turn to my left with tears, there is a desert cold

I hold out my arms to cradle, there is nothing, nothing inside

No one in front who stands

My eyes cloud over

Fogged is the sinking sky.

~~

The last few pages ripped

A pre-ordained tale nipped in the bud

An accident, a meaningless demise

The readers deprived of a possible long life

Reposing on the knoll, not a care in the world,

The protagonist.

~~

The sweltering sun high

With the easel tucked under his arm, he staggers

An ailing body, forgotten is the ward

The thought of golden hues burning in his mind,

Hunger, thirst, lust to capture the world

Near a stack of hay, a canvas fallen.

~~

Cherished you are, O Radiant One

The divine being greets you with cheer

You shine beautifully even on a moonless night,

Timeless as Horologium above

Lovelier than Cygnus

Plumes of honour more regal than the flying Pegasus

Your attire stitched with stardust

Silks flowing through the fingers like Berenice's hair.

~~

Steadfast as the mountain range beyond the fog and cloud

Unyielding as the grotto lodged within that refuses to cave in

True as the oldest of the branches of oaken trees

Stalwart as the last star that remains shining even after dawn arrives

Unfaltering like the boat that steadily weaves past the ice in the silver lake

Faithful as the bird that shall always return home…

Only upon his head would I place the circlet of gleaming gems

As blinding as his visage of steel yet his brilliant smile.

About the Author

Dibyasree Nandy

Dibyasree Nandy began writing during the lock-down period of the Covid-19 pandemic, three years ago, while pursuing the final semester of her second Master degree. She has authored fiction and short story collections, her favourite hobby being experimenting with various poetry forms. Her works have appeared in thirty-eight anthologies and literary journals.

www.ingramcontent.com/pod-product-compliance
Lightning Source LLC
LaVergne TN
LVHW041644070526
838199LV00053B/3555